A Star's Tribulation

This book was edited, formatted, designed, and published by:

UNIQUE PUBLISHING HOUSE, LLC

P.O. Box 750792, Memphis, TN 38175

www.uniquehouse.org

ISBN-10: 8803522324

ISBN-13: 9798803522324

A Star's Tribulation

Jahria L. Buford

Dedications

I dedicate this book to my mother, brother, and sisters.

Acknowledgments

Special thanks to my school E.E.S Success Academy for allowing me to write this book and my editors for helping me.

Editors: Karen Tyson & Dr. Candace Jones

1

Cruella had just had a night of fun and was now in a deep sleep. The next morning, she woke from her sleep and did her morning hygiene. As she washed her face, she tried to sing a tune from one of her songs, but it sounded horrible. She started to cry, " Oh no; my voice sounds terrible!" She knew then she would have to go to the hospital. She quickly got dressed and went to the doctor's office. He told her that her voice could possibly be permanently hoarse.

Immediately, Cruella started looking for ways to fix her hoarse voice. She asked her assistant Cleo to look also, and Cleo told her to do voice therapy. So, Cruella started voice therapy and dedicated her entire life to that. She was even drinking tea and eating things to help her. She felt devastated without being able to sing. At that point she started to search for the cause of her hoarseness.

She began by looking at the camera footage from her party. She saw her assistant Cleo standing near her cup in the video. She watched her pour something in her cup and gasped. She could not believe her eyes! She immediately started to get sad and scared because she didn't know what she could have done for Cleo to do her like that. She locked all of her doors and hid in her house.

By now, the word had gotten out all over the world about what happened to Cruella's voice. Everyone was on social media expressing how sorry they were for her. All Cruella wanted to do was to run away and never return. She didn't know what to do at that point. No matter how confused she felt, she knew that she needed to continue working on her voice , so she drank her tea.

Cruella had called her mom "Ma ,I know who did this to me!"

"Who did it baby?" her mom Pam asked.

"My assistant ma, she did this to me!" They finished their convo within ten minutes. Pam had told Cruella that she needed to inform the police about Cleo's wrongdoing. She knew her mom was right, but she just didn't know how to proceed. She was scared for her life.

Cruella spent the rest of the day chilling in bed. She cooked some food, showered , and was finally ready for bed. She went and performed her nightly beauty routine. She finally lay down in bed and slept like a baby.

The next day, two girls named Lily and Susie were passing Cruella's home. Lily looked at it and said, "Girl, did you hear about what happened to Cruella?"

"Yes, I feel so sad for her, she had a voice like an angel," said Susie.

"I wonder what the cause of it was."

"Sounds like a set up," Lilly replied. Then the two girls went on their way. Meanwhile Cruella was just sitting inside her home in a dark place. She didn't know what to do with her life.

As she sat there, she began to think of ways she could out Cleo without getting harmed again. She thought she could trust Cleo as a friend, but boy was she shocked by Cleo's evil ways. She was drinking another cup of tea and heard a buzz for the gate to be opened. Cruella grew nervous because she didn't know who was there and what was about to happen. She did not answer the buzzer because she was still scared.

Cruella had contacted her manager right after viewing the tape and let her know what she found out. Her manager asked her to get to her office immediately. Cruella got dressed and went to her manager's office. When she arrived, her manager hugged her and told her how sorry she was. She was distracted from her manager's care and concern because in the back of her mind, Cruella still wondered who had buzzed her gate.

Cruella and her manager had contacted the police. Any and everyone was now searching for Cleo. Cleo had no clue people were searching for her until she opened her phone. The news had somehow got out that Cleo was the cause of Cruella's ruined voice. Cleo had felt a wave of anger in her and called Cruella.

"I know you found out and when I find you, you're dead." Cruella had never felt so much fear in her life. She didn't know what to expect from Cleo. All she could think of was that maybe Cleo wanted money. In spite of her fears, she had the spirit to fight back. She would not let Cleo win this battle.

Cruella told her manager about the call. Her manager's office was now on lockdown. "You will be okay, don't worry about her," her manager said. But that only made Cruella more nervous. She had to do what she had to do so she could overcome this fear.

Cleo was searching around the city for Cruella while wearing a disguise. She had to kill her. She didn't understand how Cruella figured it out. She always hated how smart she was. That only made her more mad and driven to ruin Cruella.

Cleo had seen that there were a bunch of wanted signs for her on the internet. She had to leave the state, better yet the country. So, Cleo went home and packed up everything and left. She got on her secret private jet and went to Cancun. She had to hire others to execute her plans.

There was no sight of Cleo back in the US and Cruella had given up hope. She was back in her nervous stage. She then remembered she had a tracker on Cleo's phone. At this point instead of telling the police, she decided to take matters into her own hands.

2

"I need to get on the next flight to Cancun", Cruella was talking to her manager.

"You don't need to follow her, especially after what she told you, "Her manager warned her.

"I know, but I have to get to the bottom of this." Her manager pleaded with her to let the police handle this situation. Cruella had other things in mind. She had packed her things anyway. The whole time Cruella was packing, all she thought about was what she would say to Cleo. She had done so much for Cleo, and she felt betrayed. She would never understand the point of why she did it. She continuously thought and thought about what she could've done to keep this from happening. She had packed almost everything and left her house.

Cruella and her manager, with a few of her security guards, had pulled up to her private jet. "Are you sure you wanna do this?"

"Yes, nothing can change my mind." They got on the jet and Cruella was inwardly scared. No matter how afraid she was, she really felt like she had to handle this herself.

"I really hope doing this will get me the closure I need."

"You're gonna get all of the answers and closure," said her manager. Cruella began to drink her tea and prayed that everything turned out well. Things had to get better because she didn't deserve any of this. She was deep in her feelings the whole ride.

Meanwhile in Cancun, Cleo was hiring people to find Cruella. "I wonder what she's been doing, hopefully suffering." Cleo had been living the life in Cancun thinking nobody knew where she was. She sat down and really thought about how hard life had been with Cruella. She wanted Cruella to be in the background like she had been forced to be all these years.

Cruella always treated Cleo like a doormat. She barely paid her for everything she did for her, and she would pay late sometimes. She was emotionally abusive towards Cleo although it was unintentional by Cruella. Cleo was amazed that she didn't know, and she saw red. Cleo felt that all she did was to genuinely be there for Cruella; it turned to bitterness, jealousy, and hatred towards Cruella. She felt as though she had to make her experience the same pain she had gone through.

Cruella and her crew had just landed in Cancun. She was feeling lightheaded due to not eating and only drinking tea. She had grown cold feet and wanted to go back home. She felt more confident at home. She no longer wanted to go along with the confrontation, but she didn't tell anyone. Her manager tried to calm her down, not understanding her actions at the moment. Cruella now knew that she had made a huge mistake by coming to Cancun. She definitely should have thought this whole thing through. They decided they would go to the house Cruella had rented for the time they would be in Cancun. They told Cruella to sleep off her nervousness before making any decisions on what they would do. They had stopped and got something to eat first. Cruella didn't plan on getting anything, but they forced her to, since she had not eaten since they got on the plane. She'd only had tea and water. She needed to put something on her stomach so she wouldn't pass out. When they made it to their house they ate and watched TV in the dining area. Afterwards Cruella went and took a nap while the others gathered in the living room. They all started coming up with ideas on how they would move. Some ideas were smart while the others were just dumb. They knew they were in trouble for just leaving because Cruella wanted to ,instead of planning everything out.

Cruella woke from her nap and joined everyone else in the living room. "We could just rush and kill her and leave immediately after." James, one of Cruella's security guards, had said. "Why would we kill her? We would definitely go to jail! This isn't a movie, James!" Jenna shouted.

"Hey, don't be mad at me, I'm giving ideas like everyone else in the room is!" he shouted back. "Well give smart ideas instead of complete dumb ones like that!" Jenna and James went back and forth for at least five minutes giving Cruella a slight headache.

"I'm trying to understand what arguing would do to help us come up with ideas." Cruella said, slightly irritated. So, then they all decided that arguing wouldn't solve anything and got quiet. Cruella began to grow overwhelmed because she made a stupid decision by coming to Cancun. She was lost in her mind when it came to being there and was hoping someone would suggest going home so she wouldn't have to deal with all this. She had a very small piece of hope in the back of her mind. That hope wouldn't get her far enough though, or so she thought.

"I say we all write down some things we individually feel like could work and we can go from there," Mark, her main security, had spoken. Everyone else agreed and grabbed a notepad and pen and began to write down ideas. The room was silent, and everyone was in their own thoughts including Cruella. Eventually they came up with a decent plan that included some of everyone's ideas. While they were sitting there it's like something clicked in Cruella's mind and she came up with this brilliant idea to add to the plan.

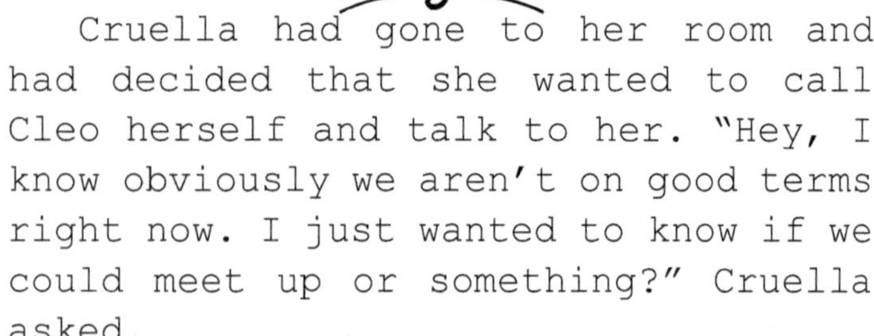

Cruella had gone to her room and had decided that she wanted to call Cleo herself and talk to her. "Hey, I know obviously we aren't on good terms right now. I just wanted to know if we could meet up or something?" Cruella asked.

"How could we meet up when you have no idea where I am?"

"We know you're in Cancun Cleo, I say let's just meet up and talk this out. It's over Cleo."

"It doesn't matter you may know where I am, but you don't have my exact location."

"You're in a beach house. I have the exact address. Cleo, if you're gonna do something to me, be smart and don't buy it in my name with my money." Cleo was in shock that Cruella had known so much so she did.

"Fine, just come!" she said and hung up in Cruella's face.

Cruella ran back downstairs excitedly and told everyone else what she had just done. Cruella and everyone else packed up everything they would need. They also packed weapons for each individual just in case things got a little wild. Jenna, Cruella's manager, didn't think the idea was safe, but she was overruled so she had to go along with it. She just didn't think meeting up with someone who tried to kill you was smart no matter how many people you showed up with. You wouldn't know what that person was capable of or what they had planned but she stuck by Cruella's side because in the end it wasn't about her. She supported her decisions as Cruella's manager and most importantly her friend.

The ride to the beach house would be a full hour drive. So, they decided it was best to rent one big truck and make it a mini road trip to keep Cruella in good spirits. They went to the rental place and rented an all-black Expedition truck and got on the road. Cruella decided that Mark would drive since he was always the main driver for Cruella. Although they attempted to make conversation with Cruella, she had a totally different thing in mind and that was getting a quick nap in. She just didn't wanna be awake to think about the situation because she was in good spirits for the moment. They all engaged in small conversations while driving to the beach house. They arrived at the house after what felt like ten hours, but it was only one.

3

They pulled into the driveway of the beach house and Mark decided to keep the truck running just in case they had to make a quick exit. Cruella had awakened once she realized they were not moving at all anymore. They didn't really wanna move until Cruella spoke, so they all just sat still in silence. Cruella looked at the house and at everyone in the truck and sighed. She pulled out her phone and called Cleo, putting the phone on speaker "Hey, we're outside, can you come out because we're definitely not coming in."

"Why would I come out when you clearly have the police out there with you," Cleo laughed because she felt as though Cruella thought she wasn't smart.

"We don't have any police out here although we should. Just come out," and with that Cruella hung up.

Cleo was sitting in the house nervous because she didn't know what she was about to walk into. She had a taser on her just in case anyone came at her. She also had a gun in her sock and one on her waist. She had to take precaution and was overly armed because Cruella did say 'us' and not just her. She put on a jacket to cover the gun on her waist and walked to the front door. She was shaking like a wet dog on the inside but sucked it up and unlocked the door. She opened the door and walked out seeing a big black tinted truck and scrunched her face up. She was wondering why she had brought such a big truck and how many people were in that truck. Cruella got out of the truck and Jenna and then James and then her other security guard Luke.

Cleo was just standing there awkwardly waiting for Cruella to talk;

she ignored everyone else. No one said anything so Cleo just decided to break the ice.

"Hey guys," she said nervously. They didn't say anything back, they just watched her closely. "Why? I just wanna know why Cleo? When I took you in when nobody else would," Cruella asked as her voice cracked. Cleo started to get frustrated as she heard Cruella play victim, well that's what she thought it was anyways. She felt like Cruella was putting on an act for her team.

Cleo started to laugh, slightly shaking her head. "Did you just have the nerve to ask why? Do you not understand what you've put me through all these years," she asked angrily? Cruella's face immediately scrunched up and a wave of confusion came upon the others also.

"What have I put you through? You have me completely lost." Cruella slightly chuckled and shook her head. Instead of answering, Cleo pulled her gun out and pointed it at Cruella.

"Move and I will blow her face off." She had seen Luke attempting to pull his gun out, but James had his weapon drawn already. Everyone's face was in shock as to why a gun was drawn.

Jenna knew this whole situation would go bad being that Cleo literally attempted to kill Cruella by poisoning her. She should have put her foot down, but at the end of the day Cruella is a grown woman.

"You don't have to do this!" shouted Jenna. Cleo was over being the bad guy when she felt as though Cruella was really the bad guy.

"Yes, I do, you don't know what's been going on. You take all the credit for my work, and she lets you and I'm sick of it." Cleo shouted. Cruella was wondering why the police weren't called because so much yelling was going on. Cruella's security guard James quickly jumped in front of her while Cleo was going off.

"Move back as I walk and quickly get in the truck," James said calmly. They both maneuvered backwards carefully.

"Why are y'all saving her? She's the villain here!" Cleo shouted while jumping up and down. She didn't shoot James because she wouldn't kill unnecessary people. She just wanted Cruella.

Jenna turned her back and started to walk to the truck also. Cruella had made it to the truck while James was still in front of her and quickly opened the door and jumped in. Jenna looked back at Cleo and said "This isn't about being a villain. It's about you needing to make better choices."

Cleo watched in envy as they did all they could to ensure not a nail on Cruella was hurt. She felt like it should be her because she did all the work, in her mind at least. They watched as she threw a mini tantrum on her porch and shook their heads. Mark quickly backed out of the driveway so they could get away from the dangerous woman. Cruella silently wondered what Cleo's issue was and why she wanted to kill her because she was genuinely confused. She thanked God for her team because without them she would've definitely been dead right now.

They drove in complete silence, scared that one or the other would say the wrong thing. Cruella was asleep as always when they would get on the road. An hour later they made it back to the house. Cruella got out of the car, unlocked the door, and went straight to her room. She lay down on her bed and just cried, still in shock at the fact that she could've lost her life just over an hour ago. She didn't understand how she had messed up; she never had ill intentions toward Cleo. She loved her like a sister and wanted the best for her, so her actions today had Cruella genuinely confused.

She felt so bad because she just wanted to help Cleo, but it seemed like she only hurt her. "Why do I always mess things up!" she shouted as she cried. She had messed things up with her biological sister and now it seemed like she was repeating history. She saw Cleo as her sister and more than an assistant, that's why she had done so much for her. Obviously, she was wrong on the sister part, because Cleo didn't even like her. Everyone else in the house had gone into their own space. They all had the same thing on their mind though and that thing was how to catch Cleo somehow.

Cruella had called her mom countless times and got no answer each time. Her mom wouldn't answer the phone and she began to grow worried. She felt like something had happened to her and she was anxious. She knew she couldn't just drive to her house like she usually would, being that she was on a whole different side of the world. She tried to call her sister, knowing she wouldn't answer, but it wasn't about her. She needed to know that her mom was okay. No one would answer the phone for her and that was stressing her out even more.

Cleo was at her beach house just sitting on the couch staring at the walls. She was just stuck in her thoughts and was mad at herself. She wanted to execute her plan so bad, but something wouldn't let her. She just couldn't see herself doing that to Cruella no matter how much she wanted to or felt like she did. She just knew in her mind that she wanted to get revenge. She had to do something to make Cruella feel like she did all these years. She just knew that she would as soon as she saw her but when Cruella got out of the car the whole plan just completely fell apart.

She just couldn't see herself hurting Cruella no matter how many times she planned and envisioned it. She just couldn't; even though Cruella deserved it by putting her through so much and playing victim. Cruella had done so much for her, and she was beyond grateful, but she didn't feel appreciated at all.

Because Cleo didn't have any family around her, Cruella was the only family she knew even though they weren't blood. She was the reason Cleo was still alive because she actually cared about her. As Cleo continued to sit and think she began to grow utterly shocked at what she had started and instantly felt guilt and regret.

Cleo felt stupid for trying to hurt the only one who was there for her. When she had nothing, Cruella believed in her and didn't mind giving up her last for her. Anyone else would've told Cleo to go get her stuff together but Cruella took her in with no hesitation. Cleo was told her whole life she would be nothing and Cruella was trying to help her become something, but all she did was push her away. She had hurt the only person who was there and that's all she could think about. She had betrayed her sister and it made her cry. She broke down on the couch and just cried for the rest of the night.

Cruella wouldn't eat or come out of her room for three days straight. She felt so sick and didn't want to be bothered with anyone. They had one week left in Cancun and she was ready to leave now. No one had heard from Cruella's family no matter whose phone had called them. She was so bothered and worried because she felt as though Cleo had done something to them as a part of her plan to get back at her. She didn't care about catching Cleo anymore; she needed her mom. She wouldn't be okay until she knew her mom was okay.

Cruella was literally drained and felt as though tons of bricks were laying on her. She didn't know what to do and it really wasn't anything she could do until she got back to the United States.

Life was going so great two months ago and everything had just come tumbling down at one time. She had lost so much in a short amount of time and now she felt like she was losing herself completely. She was ready to give up and just disappear and focus on herself, but she knew she couldn't because she had too many people depending on her.

Cruella began to feel like maybe she deserved this. All of the bad things that came to her she felt like she deserved , because she was always unintentionally hurting people around her when in reality, she only wanted to make them happy. She had been beating herself up since Cleo told her what she did about hurting her, and she couldn't stop. She started to blame herself for everything that was happening to her. She just wanted everything to go right and everyone around her to be happy. She just wanted all the hurt to end and experience a bundle of happiness. She just lay there in silence not wanting to move.

4

The day had finally come for them to leave Cancun. Cruella had got up early and packed all of her things. She was ready to get to her mom and make sure everything was okay. Everyone else was still getting their things together so Cruella just stayed in her room and cleaned up after herself. They hadn't had any more contact with Cleo while they were there, not even a phone call or anything else. It was like she had disappeared off the face of the Earth because she wasn't at the beach house anymore. Cruella had received an email saying that Cleo had checked out. Cruella got every notification because Cleo paid for it in her name and with her credit card. She had access to her accounts because she was still considered to be Cruella's assistant.

Cruella eventually came out and brought all of her belongings to the front of the house. They all made sure to clean the house and fix it up to how it was. It didn't take long because they didn't make a mess in the house. They started taking their things and packed them outside in the SUV. Cruella went into the house and made sure everything was in order before she locked the front door and put the key into the mailbox and got in the truck. Mark made sure everyone was settled and started the truck and pulled out. The ride to the airport was quiet, everyone was in their own world. Of course, as usual Cruella was asleep.

Mark pulled up to the airport and drove to the back and pulled up to the private jet. They all got out and the men grabbed the bags and put them on the jet. Cruella was climbing the stairs to get on the jet and a car pulled up fast. Cruella's security James had hurried her into the jet and walked back out. She looked out of the window and saw it was Cleo. She looked like she was panicking and kept pointing towards the jet gesturing towards Cruella. Cruella couldn't hear anything she was saying but it had to be about her because she kept pointing. Shortly after everyone else got on the jet and sat in their seats. Cleo got back in her car and pulled off and they took off.

Cruella was quiet as they took off and got up and went to the bedroom that was on the jet. She was waiting on one of them to tell her what Cleo wanted but they never did so she went to the bedroom. She didn't even understand how Cleo had found them; she was confused. No one was talking to her because she had been ignoring them up until it was time to go; everyone except Jenna, that is. They didn't like how she was treating them when they were there for her.

Jenna noticed the confused look on Cruella's face before she went to the room, so she followed. "She came because she claimed she wanted to apologize." Cruella truly believed that, but she wanted to know how she found them or knew they would be here today.

"I mean that's cool but how did she know we were here?" She looked at Jenna waiting to hear her answer with a confused facial expression.

"She said she saw the SUV and decided to follow us because she needed to speak with you." Cruella was still confused about the situation, but she understood they put her in the jet for her safety.

They had finished up their conversation and decided to lay on the bed and relax. Cruella couldn't seem to stop thinking about the situations that had been transpiring in her life. From dealing with the dangerous Cleo to her family not responding to her, she was beyond stressed. She couldn't wait to get back home so she could find them and hopefully find them alive and well. She felt like she was too deep in her thoughts, so she decided to take a quick nap. She eventually awoke from her nap and just laid there watching YouTube on her phone. Shortly after the plane ride they had arrived back home, and Cruella was the most excited she had been in months but also nervous.

Cruella had gotten off the plane and put her things in her vehicle and drove home. She arrived home and showered and took care of her hygiene. She finished and fixed herself something to eat. She thought about driving to her mom's house but decided to take a quick nap before she went. She awoke from her nap, brushed her teeth and left her house to go to her mother's house.

She got in her car and started it and sat there for a quick minute. She said a quick prayer hoping that she would arrive to find her mother safe and had just had her phone powered off. She really wanted her mom to be okay and safe. She thought about past mistakes and called her manager.

"Hey, I'm heading to my mom's house. I was wondering if you could come with me for safety purposes?"

Jenna knew this would happen but didn't expect it literally the day they returned. "Yes, I'm on my way now."

Cruella sat there and waited for Jenna to arrive so they could leave. She had also called her main security Mark for protection. They both arrived shortly, and Mark had told Cruella to let him drive. They all got comfortable in her car and put on seat belts.

"Why can't you just let the police handle something for you Cruella?" Jenna asked, genuinely concerned. Cruella felt like nobody understood her motives. It was her family being involved that took a totally different toll on things.

"I can't do something like that when it involves family. I have to make sure firsthand that my mom is okay."

Mark had started the car and began the route to her mom's house. The rest of the way there they were quiet. They eventually made it and they all sat there to see who would make the first move to get out of the car. Nobody would get out of the car because they didn't know what they would walk into on the inside of the house.

"Are we gonna go in or what? Cruella , you wanted to come here so what are you waiting for?" Mark asked.

"We will go in once I'm ready. Can I brace myself?" she shouted. Mark started to grow irritated and was getting ready to pull off.

Shortly after, Cruella got out of the car and Jenna and Mark followed after her. They all got to the front door and Cruella took her keys out and looked back at them nervously. She slowly unlocked the door, and her hands shook while doing it. She began to open the door and continued to shake trying to prepare herself for anything that could happen. She stepped into the house with a look of confusion and shock. Mark and Jenna stepped in and gasped at the sight, slightly confused.

"Mom! Are you home?" They walked towards the living room still confused about what was going on. They walked through the entire house searching for her mom. Cruella was still calling her but wasn't getting any reply. The entire house was empty and clean with no trace of her mom. There was no furniture anywhere, not even a refrigerator in sight. Cruella slid down on the wall and cried trying to control her emotions. She wanted to know where her mom was. She was definitely losing her mind; this was the last strike.

She continued to cry while sitting on the ground not knowing what to do.

"Where is my mom?" she repeated every couple of seconds. Mark just stood there in pain for her feeling bad that there was nothing he could do to help her right now. Jenna immediately sat next to her and comforted her with hugs, and she also shed some tears too, sad at the fact that Cruella kept going through things.

"Cruella at this point we have to call the police," Jenna said while hugging her. Cruella ignored her and continued to cry, not even worried about the police. She eventually got up and walked out of the door and slammed it shut. She got back in her car and stared at the house in tears completely numb.

Mark and Jenna came out shortly after, sad for Cruella.

"Cruella, can you come lock the door?" Jenna asked. Cruella tossed the keys to her and laid her head on the window slightly frustrated that things weren't going right. Mark got in the car as Jenna locked the door. Jenna got in also and he started the car.

"We're gonna find her Cruella, I promise you, if it's the last thing I do," Mark said to her. He reached back and rubbed her shoulder in a comforting manner. Jenna disagreed silently; she felt like they should involve the police because it was too dangerous. Mark pulled out of the driveway and drove off.

They drove Cruella to get something to eat because she hadn't eaten since they left. She decided that she wanted to get a salad from Chick-Fil-A. They drove her home and stayed so she could have company. They felt like she needed someone with her so she wouldn't make dumb decisions. They all made it in the house and sat in the theater room watching a movie while eating. They all froze when they heard a knock at the door.

5

They all sat in silence while still eating hoping the knocking would eventually go away. Another minute had passed, and the knocking continued. Mark grew frustrated because it was always something happening. They were trying to figure out how someone got in the gate to be able to knock on the door in the first place. Mark put his food aside and left the room to see who was at the door and what they wanted. Cruella stayed seated not wanting to go out in case of an emergency. When she heard Mark slightly raise his voice, she walked out to the front to see what was happening.

As she got to the front, she heard her mom begging to come in. She was confused about how they were just at her house, and it was empty, but she showed up shortly afterwards at her house.

"Please let me in, I've been waiting for her to get back," Mark just listened to her vent and felt that it was crap because she should have reached out before now. He didn't know whether to trust her or not because her actions have been sketchy. In this time anyone could have intentions to hurt Cruella and he wasn't gonna allow it any longer.

"Hold on stay right here," Mark said while sighing.

Mark had turned and saw Cruella standing there. She guessed he was coming to tell her that her mom was there.

"Should I let her in? I will turn her around if you don't want her here." Cruella wanted to get answers, but she couldn't trust her mom at this point. She didn't know what she had going on. "No, I've been blowing her up and she's been ignoring me, now she wants to show up." Mark shook his head because he wanted an explanation, but he couldn't force Cruella to make her come into her house. He also didn't want to just lock her mom out because he had respect for her, but he had to respect Cruella's wishes. He walked back to the door and opened it.

"Sorry she doesn't want to see you." He closed the door and felt bad. It felt like he was shutting the door in his own mother's face.

Mark locked the door and they all walked back to the theater room. Cruella felt some type of way and she kind of felt bad. She had to put herself first because she hadn't been doing that. She wondered why her mom showed up after ignoring her and not telling her that she moved. Jenna asked, "Who was at the door?" She had chosen to stay seated while they went to the door.

"No one important," Mark replied quickly.

Jenna looked at the both of them suspiciously; they seemed like they were up to something. Everyone looked towards the door as they heard knocking again.

"Bro what do your mom want now," Mark said irritated as he got up.

"Wait, that was her mom, why won't you let her in?" Jenna asked. Cruella looked at her like she was crazy.

"We can't trust her look at what she did," Cruella said. Her mom started knocking hard on the door like she was demanding to be let in.

Jenna wanted to know why she was here, so she said, "Let's just go see what she wants." They all agreed so they walked out of the theater room and to the front. Jenna decided to open the door this time and saw Pam, Cruella's mom, crying her eyes out. When Cruella saw her mom crying, she began to feel bad for not letting her in the first time.

"I just want to talk to my daughter, that's it please and then I'll leave," Pam cried out. Cruella decided to invite her mom in and hugged her apologizing for not letting her in the first time.

Pam had been in the house for twenty minutes and she felt happy to be in her daughter's presence again. They had just been catching up with each other about things that had been going on.

"Why weren't you answering my calls when I was calling?" She looked at her mom trying to figure out if she would be honest.

"I didn't have the money to pay my bill, and also I was evicted because I couldn't pay my bills." Cruella's face grew shocked and kind of hurt that she didn't try to find a way to communicate that with her.

"You should have said something mom you know I would've helped out immediately." They finished up their conversation within thirty minutes.

Cruella had told her mom she could stay at her house. She would feel even worse if she put her out and plus it was her mom. She had bags of clothes and shoes with her, so they helped her bring them in. They took her things to a guest room and gave her space until she settled in. They went into the living room and sat on the couch.

"Why do y'all think she's really here?" Jenna asked. She was the one that wanted to let her in, but she also questioned her motives.

"I don't know but me and you are staying until she leaves, or we feel that we can trust her for Cruella's safety," Mark said.

Cruella just didn't understand how to start her conversation with her mom about why she was really here.

"What should I say to her? It's never been awkward with her, she's, my mom." Jenna completely understood where Cruella was coming from because it should never be awkward to talk to your parents.

"I think you should ask about her and everyone else disappearing and also ask how she got here," Jenna said. Mark agreed heavily on how she got here because there is no way she walked alone at that.

"I really don't want her here until I feel like I can trust her again, but I don't know if that will ever happen but she's my mom and has nowhere else to go."

Mark and Jenna knew where she was coming from. Her mom's safety was being put first even before her own.

"You have every right to kick her out if you want to because your safety comes first, but I understand."

Shortly after her mom came into the living room, she was ready for the questions. She had changed into clothes more comfortable and relaxed on the couch. She was more so ready to talk to Cruella because she knew Cruella didn't really want her here. She had so many things on her mind and so much more to say. She was also feeling some type of way at the fact that she was considering people who weren't even actual family opinions. She felt betrayed by her daughter in a way.

Cruella had thought about how to approach her mom without being completely rude. Her mom was one of her weak spots and could easily get over on Cruella because of her role. She could easily be persuaded by just a sentence that came out of her mom's mouth. Seeing her mom outside of her home after ignoring her for so long was kind of a relief. Cruella was just happy to know she wasn't harmed or dead.

Cruella went and freshened up before going to talk to her mom. She had showered, brushed her teeth, and put on comfortable clothes. She was getting ready to go have the conversation with her and was acting as if it was a big deal. She was practicing things she would say and how she would say it to her without being rude. Nothing she thought of sounded good to say to her mom but at the end of the day she had to express herself and she was going to do it. She walked out of her room and towards the room her mom was staying in. As she approached the door and began to knock her mom opened the door with the exact same thing on her mind. It was funny to them both how they thought alike. Well, this was an urgent conversation if Pam would be staying anyways.

They both smiled at the fact that they were doing the same thing and had the same thoughts in their minds.

"Wow we really are alike in a way" Cruella agreed silently but also thought this would happen anyways because it was on her mind heavily. She continued to smile lightly, not trying to give off a smart tone or negative atmosphere for the conversation. Pam opened her room door wide for Cruella to come in and closed it after she did. When Cruella had entered the room, she looked at all of Pam's things and sat down on the edge of the bed. Cruella started to panic on the inside, not really ready to talk but this had to happen in order for Pam to stay at her house. Pam decided she would start the conversation once she realized Cruella wasn't going to.

"First I would like to apologize because my actions were completely childish and wrong." She started off and knew that wouldn't get her far, but she meant it. "My intentions were never to hurt your feelings or hurt you period. I just didn't want to be a burden to you for once, you know." Cruella looked down listening to her mother rant understanding in a way where she was coming from. "I just wanted you to be proud of me like you have always made me proud, you know." Cruella immediately felt like her mom felt like she failed, "Mom I will always be proud of you for the simple fact that you raised me and my siblings the best you could. You sacrificed so much for us to live a good life and we will forever cherish that. If you ever need anything don't hesitate to call on me," Cruella finished

Pam agreed silently, "I know but that still doesn't justify me not having my stuff together." Cruella again shook her head disagreeing because everyone went through things. Nobody's life would ever be perfect.

"You always tried your best and if I knew about anything you were going through you would've been here with me or in your own place. You deserve the world and more, you're an amazing selfless mom. I'm sorry for not even realizing something was wrong and seeing if you were good financially." Cruella had hugged her mom after saying that and Pam had said something that caught her completely off guard.

"Cleo wanted me to help her."

6

Cruella had been completely caught off guard with that statement from her mom.

"Wait, you said Cleo wanted you to do what now?" Cruella asked loudly. Cruella began to hyperventilate as she thought about the possibility of her mom turning on her.

"Yes, she wanted me to work for her to harm you; of course, I said no," Pam stated immediately. Pam immediately felt bad although she didn't do it and gave Cleo a mouthful for even having the guts to call her to hurt her own daughter. She couldn't believe Cleo was serious at first until she further explained and was immediately told 'no' and blocked from contacting Pam. She wanted to know what made her think she would harm her own daughter for money when money could never replace relationships.

Cruella began to put things together in her head and made a big realization. If Pam knew Cleo's plan all along, why she acted surprised when Cruella called and let her know what Cleo had done to her. She had already known Cleo was planning something against her so why did she do that?

"Mom, if you knew Cleo was planning to hurt me, why didn't you tell me?" Pam didn't even have a reasonable answer for Cruella; she didn't even know herself. She couldn't think of any reasons on why she didn't tell her daughter someone was out to get her. Cruella's feelings were beyond hurt to hear this information from her own mother. She couldn't even trust her mom in her home anymore because what if this was a complete act.

"Cruella, I wanted to, but I just didn't know how. Especially when you told me she poisoned you. I felt so guilty knowing I could've prevented it." Cruella didn't even care to hear her talk anymore because it could have all been a lie at that point. She stormed out of the room and went to her own room. She had nothing else to say to her mom at the moment.

Cruella stayed in her room for the rest of that day with the door locked. She wasn't feeling anyone or anything and wanted to be left alone. She felt like she couldn't trust anyone anymore after something like this had happened. Her own mother basically betrayed her and didn't tell her something that could've prevented her attack. The major thing was Cruella had told her mom what happened and who did it and she acted as if she was so shocked but knew all along something was being planned to harm her. She was done letting people run over her, she couldn't take that anymore.

Cruella heard a light knock on her door and rolled her eyes. She ignored it and continued to watch tv because she didn't want to see or talk to anyone. At the moment she only wanted her space. The person decided to knock again after getting ignored and Cruella screamed "WHAT!". The person didn't say anything, so Cruella got out of bed and opened the door. She thought it would be her mother since the person didn't respond when she said what, but it was only Jenna. She opened her door wider for her to walk in and closed the door locking it back.

It was quiet for a minute until Cruella began to cry.

"I just can't believe my mom knew and said nothing. I just can't grasp that in my head." Cruella cried in Jenna's arms. Jenna just held her as she vented because that was all she could do. She completely understood Cruella.

"Like how my own mother could keep something so big from me when she knew Cleo had access to me and everything around me."

Jenna continued to comfort her while listening and decided to say, "I know, and I am here for you Cruella. Some people just choose not to do the right things because they feel like they have a better solution." Cruella had gotten quiet as she listened to

Jenna tell her the right things to calm her completely and felt that she was right about everything.

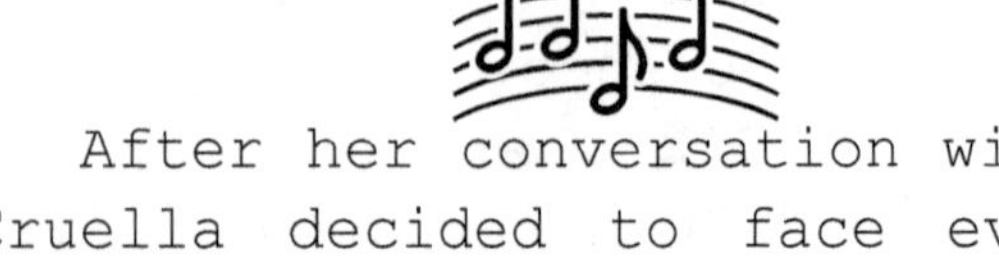

After her conversation with Jenna, Cruella decided to face everything. She had finally come out of her room after a day or two. She could genuinely say she was in a better mood and felt good today and wondered how long that would last.

"Jenna I'm actually feeling better today," she said as she entered the living room. She didn't see her like she usually would and frowned wondering why she didn't tell her she was leaving. Cruella didn't want to be home with her mom alone at all even if Mark was there. She quickly walked to the kitchen and got a cereal bar and water bottle. She then walked back to her room so she wouldn't come in contact with her mom.

When she got back to her room she quickly closed and locked her door. She called Jenna on her phone, "Why didn't you say you were leaving? I would've left with you!" Jenna on the other line was confused on what Cruella was talking about.

"I haven't left, I'm literally outside in the pool." Cruella immediately felt bad for assuming instead of asking. She was just nervous. She decided she would also go down to the pool to get some fresh air and sunlight.

"Oh, my bad I thought you were gone because it was so quiet and you would usually be making yourself breakfast, I'll be down there soon," she hung the phone up.

Cruella turned on her room light and began to get ready for the pool. She had put on a black and white two piece and put her hair in a bun just in case she actually decided to get in the water. She put on sunscreen and got a towel and grabbed her phone from her bed. As she was walking out of her room, her mom looked as if she was about to knock.

"Oh, you're leaving?" Pam asked, wanting to talk to Cruella.

"No, I'm just going down to the pool to get some fresh air." She walked past her mom not waiting for her response and went down to the pool with Jenna.

Cruella had made it down to the pool in her backyard feeling the sun on her skin. She saw Jenna, James, and Mark all in the pool talking and laughing and smiled because she loved her team. She walked to the steps and slowly began to walk down into the pool.

"Woah it's cold in here," she said while shivering. They looked at her and laughed at how she was shivering.

"Yeah, I said the same thing, but why are you shaking like that?" Mark asked while laughing at her. She shrugged while laughing also and floated over to them.

They stayed in the pool and joked around for about an hour and a half just enjoying each other's company. The men went in the house to shower while Jenna and Cruella stayed outside and laid on the chairs by the pool to dry off a bit. They both just laid in silence enjoying the heat from the sun.

"So have you talked to your mom since the other day?" Jenna asked while looking over at Cruella. Cruella knew Jenna would wanna talk about that and although she really didn't, she answered.

"Actually, no I haven't, she was about to try before I came down, but I was already on my way down here and I really don't feel like talking to her right now especially about that."

They finished their conversation about nothing really, just catching up. They enjoyed having girl time and felt like they were getting closer since Jenna practically lived with Cruella now. After they both were dry, they got up and went into the house and into their own rooms. Cruella decided to take a shower and clean up around the house a bit because she was bored. She walked into the kitchen and started wiping everything down and washing dishes. As she was cleaning, her mom came and sat down watching her.

"Mom, I know you wanted to talk but I'm not ready so we will talk when I feel like I'm ready." Cruella continued to clean, and her mom sighed while going back to her room.

Cruella laid in her bed scrolling on her social media and laughing at random videos. She felt so relaxed and in a good mood like she had started feeling every day. She wanted to get out of the house and do something, but Jenna and Mark told her it wasn't smart to do because she didn't know who could be watching her. So, she agreed and decided she would just stay home and chill as usual. It was extremely boring though and she needed to find something to do to stay productive. She felt like cooking so she went to the kitchen and took out the ingredients she would need.

She decided she would settle with eating taco salad, so she began to make the taco meat because that was the only thing she actually needed to cook. She actually loved to cook but never had the time to because she was usually always out or busy. She finished preparing the meat and decided this was a time she could use to talk to her mom. She walked to her mom's room and knocked on the door.

"Mom, I made food if you're hungry." She then went back to the kitchen and started making her plate. Pam had come in shortly after and spoke to Cruella and washed her hands. She began making her plate also and filled it up because she loved taco salad. She also loved when Cruella made food because that was another one of her talents. When they both finished making their plates they sat down and started eating.

"Mom, I forgive you and I still love you. I just don't like how you went about the situation." Pam agreed one hundred percent and did not question Cruella's words and she also apologized. They hugged it out and continued to eat while making small talk about nothing.

7

Cleo was still in Cancun trying to figure out how she would manage to get another conversation out of Cruella. She couldn't call because Cruella's phone went straight to voicemail and so did everyone else's around her. She had to vent and get closure before she made the big decision she had planned. She was ready for everything to be over and just go on about her life even if it meant jail time. She had finally come to her senses to give up the villain act and make things right.

She had to figure out how she would get back home without being sighted.

Being that she was still technically wanted, she couldn't just go back home. She had left the beach house just in case Cruella tried to call the cops on her and went to a nice hotel. Though everything was nice in Cancun she was ready to return home. She was very homesick and felt lonely and abandoned.

She decided she would come up with a plan to get back home. She had called many of her connections and fellow criminal friends to help her. She wanted to disguise herself so she wouldn't be detected but it would be hard. She made herself a fake I.D and did many things to change herself. She was soon prepared to go back home. She checked out of her hotel room and got all of her things to get on a private jet she rented with Cruella's money. She was on her way back home to make things right.

Cleo was nearly at home. She was the happiest yet the most nervous she had ever been. She couldn't believe that the plan she came up with in only a couple of hours had come together. She had made no contact with the police since she had got on the jet. To kill time, she was planning out how she would get everything together with Cruella and not in a violent way. She was ready to finally face her fears and be mature because she was too grown to be acting like this.

She wished she would have just communicated with Cruella how she felt from the beginning instead of doing the stuff she did. What made her really come to her senses was that Cruella seemed confused and like she didn't know she had been hurting Cleo. That made Cleo feel ten times worse because it could have been fixed with one simple conversation. Now that it was definitely too late, Cleo felt so stupid for her actions. She just wished she had a time machine to go back and right her wrongs.

She eventually made it back home and kept her disguise on for safety purposes. She drove a car one of her connections left for her back home. When she made it home it was still in order because no one knew where she lived, so it was safe. She showered and ate and took a quick nap. She needed as much rest as possible to prepare for the storm she would soon be facing.

The next morning Cleo began writing letters to everyone she encountered while working for Cruella. She was writing apology letters and expressing things she never had although she should have. She felt like things would be better and easier if she included them also because they were a part of her life and went through the pain with Cruella. She felt like she owed it to them to do things in a good and peaceful way.

As she was writing Cruella's letter, she began to cry silently as she poured her heart out. It felt like she was writing a goodbye letter and although technically it was, it was weird. She didn't want to say goodbye or be away from someone she saw as a sister, but it was needed for everything to be okay again. She had to suffer major consequences for her actions. Even if it meant spending the rest of her life in jail.

She wrapped up all of the letters and placed them in envelopes. She had packaged them in a nice bag and wrapped them. She had planned to take it to Cruella's house where we would hopefully have one more conversation. She felt like some of the pressure was off her when she wrote those letters. She still felt heavy from the nervousness about facing Cruella.

Cruella had awakened from her sleep in the middle of the night. Cleo was heavy on her mind, and she couldn't understand why when things weren't good. She just hoped things were good with her and that she wasn't in any type of danger. She had gotten up and decided to say a quick prayer for her and became emotional while doing so. She just wanted things to be okay for everybody, although she knew things wouldn't end that way unfortunately. She wished she could go back and just be there for her like Cleo needed and wanted.

She eventually went back to sleep and had a strange dream about Cleo which completely weirded her out. She had dreamed that Cleo was back home and in danger, but she couldn't understand how she could be back at home when she wasn't notified about any of her accounts being used. Maybe Cleo had found someone else to bring her home because there was no way she came freely without being caught by the police. She awoke from her sleep again and grew confused as to why her only thoughts were of Cleo. She decided to get up and not go back to sleep because she didn't want to have another weird dream or to dream at all. She decided to get a journal and write a letter to Cleo even if she never saw her again and began to write down everything she felt on the paper.

The first thing she did was apologize about neglecting her feelings and not being attentive like she should have been. She didn't do it purposefully and felt like things were great between the two because Cleo seemed happy. She talked about good memories they had together and created because they've known each other for over six years. They also shared a lot of memories because they basically traveled the whole world together because her assistant went wherever she went. Cruella cried once she finally finished writing and felt a huge relief come over her. By the time she had gotten herself together, it was morning and time to get up.

Cruella decided to get up, shower, and go chat with Jenna wherever she was. She left her room and smelled food, so she knew Jenna was in the kitchen making breakfast for everyone. Mark and Jenna decided to move in temporarily until they felt Pam was safe enough to be around Cruella alone or until Cruella felt comfortable because right now, she didn't.

"Morning, what are you cooking?" Cruella asked while sitting in a chair near the island in the kitchen.

"Oh, I'm just making omelets and steaks for everyone. I will probably make some pancakes also. How'd you sleep last night though," Jenna noticed bags under Cruella's eyes and knew she probably didn't get any sleep.

Cruella sighed knowing she looked very tired, so it was easy to point out she had gotten no sleep the previous night.

"I slept terribly. I couldn't get Cleo off my mind. I feel like she's in some type of danger."

Jenna sighed, not wanting Cruella to worry about her anymore. She felt like Cruella should leave that in the past and make good memories with the things that's going on now so she wouldn't stress herself out.

"Sorry to hear that, but I say leave thoughts of her alone. She deserves whatever is coming to her honestly." Cruella wanted to agree and feel that exact way towards Cleo also, but she just didn't have it in her heart because she saw her as her sister.

"Yeah, I know."

The conversation was interrupted by a knock at the door and it kind of made Cruella jump. The two of them looked towards the door and at each other wondering who it could be early this morning, maybe Luke or James the other security but they had keys. It was obvious that it was someone who knew the gate code because they were at the front door and not buzzing the gate. Mark had come from the back and spoke to the two women before opening the door without checking. His face had

grown completely shocked at who was
facing him at the front door.

8

Mark was stuck in a trance for a while before asking the person what they were doing there.

"I'm here to talk to Cruella before I leave for good," the voice said.

Cruella's heart had begun to beat four hundred miles per hour at who she heard. She immediately grew scared for her life and wanted to disappear.

"You need to leave before we call the cops. Why did you think it was okay to show up here today?" Mark yelled.

They had already figured out that it was Cleo and were irritated.

"I'm already gonna turn myself in and hopefully Cruella can heal from this and in a way me too," Cleo said while tearing up.

Cruella nodded her head at Mark for him to let her in and walked to her room. She felt so heavy and needed to brace herself for this whole conversation they would soon have. She just couldn't believe Cleo had the boldness to show up to her house or even come back home while being wanted by the law.

She had gotten herself together and walked back to the front. She looked and saw Cleo standing by the wall and invited her to follow her. Mark and Jenna began to go against that because they didn't trust Cleo alone with her. Cruella told them she would be fine and walked to her office. She invited Cleo in and closed the door. They both sat down and stared at everything but each other.

They had both begun talking to each other at the same time and stopped. Cleo had begun by telling Cruella everything she felt like she endured while working for her. She also apologized in every other sentence not even realizing she was saying it too much. Cleo continued to vent her entire heart out to Cruella. She had begun to cry while talking too because she felt so overwhelmed that she could finally express herself.

Mark had come and stood by the door not to listen to their conversation but to be there just in case. He couldn't let anything else happen to Cruella while she was in his care and on duty to protect her.

Pam had noticed him there and began to question him on who was here. Mark had simply dismissed her and told her they would talk about it later if Cruella wanted to tell her. He hoped Cleo didn't have any ill intentions in her mind towards Cruella.

While in the office, Cleo and Cruella were still expressing everything they felt that was needed to talk about. It was now Cruella's turn and she cried almost immediately while trying to explain her wrong doings. She had never meant to do anything but love and be there for Cleo, but Cleo saw the exact opposite. She realized that people always said that about her and it didn't sit right with her because she didn't feel like she was hurting anybody. Cruella had told her that all she had to do was come to her and say something, so they could've fixed it and moved on in a positive manner. She told her how she saw her as her sister and that she felt like they were super close. She felt terrible and also kept apologizing a million times.

They talked for a whole three hours non-stop, and they both felt like stress was coming off of them. They had cried, yelled, laughed, and hugged so much that it felt like everything was going back to normal. They had missed each other so much but they knew it would soon come to an end and that dampened the mood completely. Cleo had told her that she would be turning herself in and was willing to face her consequences. Cruella objected and said she would drop all charges and get Cleo help, but Cleo declined. Everything couldn't get looked over and she had to do her time. She wanted to right her wrongs.

Cleo had given Cruella the bag she had all the wrapped letters in and told her not to open it until she was gone. Cruella obeyed and also gave her the journal she wrote about her to read before she turned herself in. She couldn't believe this is how things would end when it didn't have to end that way. She wished there was something she could do to change Cleo's mind but there was nothing she could do. Cleo was stuck on her own decision. She couldn't force Cleo to not turn herself in because it was her life. She promised to always visit and be there for her no matter what.

Cleo was her sister no matter if they were blood or not. They would forever be sisters. They both walked out of the office and back into the living room where everyone else was. Luke and James had come over when Mark informed them that Cleo had showed up that morning. Cleo had apologized to everyone in the house including Pam, especially for trying to turn her against her own daughter. She had told everyone what she was planning to do, and they tried to change her mind, but she declined. She picked up her phone and called the police on herself. She gave them her location and they were on their way immediately when they realized where she was. Everyone in the house waited for the cops with Cleo and Cruella both sobbing and Jenna shedding tears, sad that this was the ending of a six-year sister bond.

Shortly after, the police arrived at the gate and Cruella hesitated before she opened it with tears in her eyes. She begged the police to be gentle with Cleo, but they were ready to take her into custody. There were so many cops' cars you would think they were stopping a heist or a shootout. Cruella continued to cry as she opened the door completely and they ordered Cleo away from Cruella and on the ground. They hugged one last time and she got on the ground with her hands on her head with tears in her eyes. They put her in handcuffs and read her her rights listing off all the things she was getting arrested for. Cruella had felt like she was in a movie and that the event taking place in front of her wasn't really happening.

They had taken her outside and Cruella shouted I love you to Cleo and for her to be safe as they put her in the car. Cleo immediately responded with the same words crying, not ready but ready to face her fate. They had driven out of the gate and the news spread quickly all over the internet of what took place. Cleo had gotten arrested and was in custody after calling the police on herself while being at Cruella's estate.

Cruella was crushed and still in so much shock that she hadn't even gone back into the house yet. Pam was crushed for her daughter and went to comfort her, but Cruella had pushed away from her and went back into the house dashing to her room extremely emotional. She locked herself in there and cried and cried until she could barely breathe anymore. She had noticed the bag of letters Cleo gave her while they were talking and got up to open it and retrieved her letter. She opened it and read it and began crying at how genuine and heartwarming it was. She felt like Cleo had poured out her heart into the letter. Cruella would probably never recover from this.

Months later Cruella had gotten into counseling to help her with her emotions. She had completely lost herself after the whole incident and felt completely traumatized. She had been slightly better but still needed time to recover for her sake. She had decided that she didn't want to be in the limelight anymore because it was a very toxic environment. She had retired from music completely and wanted to live her life for her like she should have been doing. She had begun to put herself first no matter who the person was.

She had sold her home and moved into something more secluded and small so people wouldn't be in her space. She had retired her mom and moved her into a small condo and took care of her financially because she deserved it and she wanted to. Mark was still her security and would come out with her whenever she requested but he was more like her big brother. Jenna was no longer her manager because she didn't need one anymore since she retired. Jenna deserved the title and proved it even though she didn't ask for it.

Cleo was in prison still waiting for her trial to begin and it was extremely stressful and quite frustrating. Cruella visited her every chance she could and put money on her books. Cleo would be set for life if she would have to spend the rest of it in jail according to Cruella. Everything was starting to fall into place in life for both women even though they were both still slightly traumatized. Cruella was just happy that she was still alive, and no one involved was dead or hurt during the situation. She was ready to live life and do everything she never thought she would or could be able to. She was happy that she overcame all her tribulations as a star.

About the Author

Jahria L. Buford is a seventeen-year-old high school senior who attends EES Success Academy.

www.ingramcontent.com/pod-product-compliance
Lightning Source LLC
Chambersburg PA
CBHW061332120726
48001CB00002B/813